BIRDS OF A FEATHER

HarperFestival is an imprint of HarperCollins Publishers.

Rio: Birds of a Feather

For information address HarperCollins Children's Books, a division of HarperCollins Publishers, 10 East 53rd Street, New York, NY 10022.
www.harpercollinschildrens.com
Library of Congress catalog card number: 2010933167
ISBN 978-0-06-202267-7
Book design by Rick Farley.
11 12 13 14 15   CWM   10 9 8 7 6 5 4 3 2 1
❖
First edition

Rio

BIRDS OF a FEATHER

Adapted by Susan Korman
Based on the motion picture screenplay
by Todd R. Jones and Earl Richey Jones

HARPER FESTIVAL
An Imprint of HarperCollinsPublishers

One day a mysterious stranger entered Linda's bookstore. "Can I help you?" asked Linda.

The man stared right at Blu. "I'd like to see your bird."

With a frightened squawk, Blu rushed for his cage.

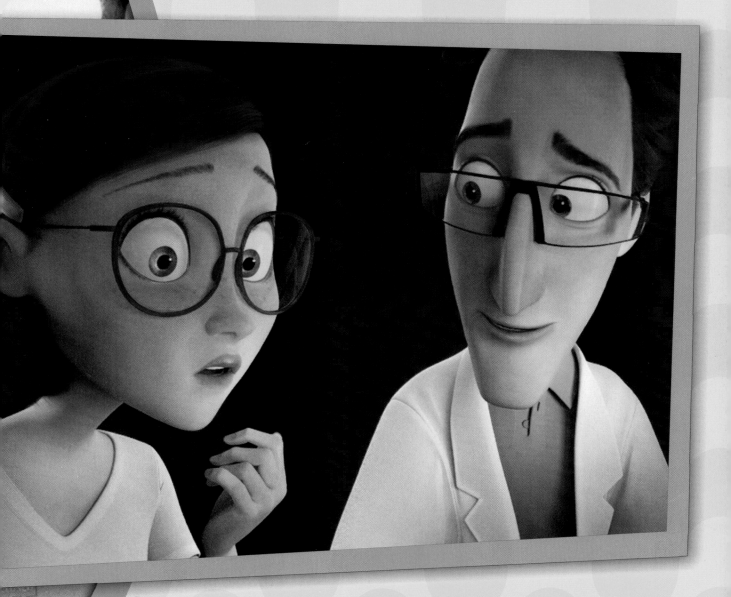

The man was a bird scientist named Tulio. He told Linda that Blu was the last male blue Spix's Macaw in the world.

"He's a special bird," Tulio said. "We must take him to Rio to meet a female blue Spix's Macaw. Her name is Jewel."

Blu and Linda didn't want to leave Minnesota, but they finally agreed to go. When they arrived in Rio, everyone was on the beach. Blu had never seen anything like it!

At the Conservation Center, Tulio showed them some sick birds that he was taking care of. Many had been rescued from dangerous smugglers. He also introduced Blu to Jewel.

Blu had been nervous about meeting Jewel—until he saw her. *Whoa,* he thought. *She's beautiful!* But Blu quickly learned that Jewel wasn't very friendly.

When Jewel spotted Blu in her cage, she flew down and pinned him to the floor. "What are you doing here?" she demanded.

Meanwhile Marcel, a bird smuggler, was plotting to steal the two valuable macaws. Marcel sent his evil cockatoo, Nigel, and his young friend, Fernando, to kidnap them.

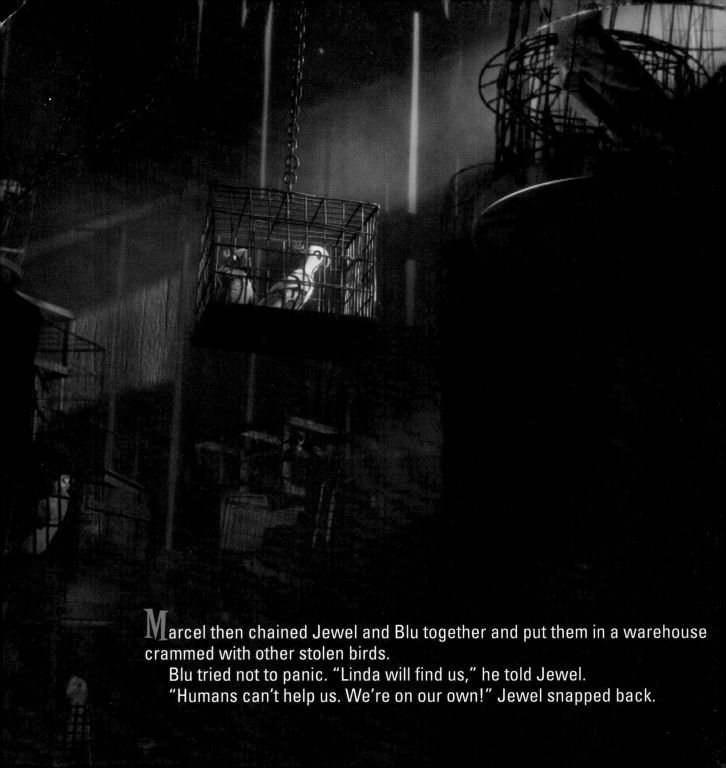

Marcel then chained Jewel and Blu together and put them in a warehouse crammed with other stolen birds.

Blu tried not to panic. "Linda will find us," he told Jewel.

"Humans can't help us. We're on our own!" Jewel snapped back.

Jewel rocked the cage back and forth, trying to smash it open. Finally, Blu just slid open the lock.

"Help! Save us!" cried the other birds from their cages.
Blu and Jewel wanted to free them, but then Nigel flew to their cage.

Luckily, they escaped. "Come on!" Jewel flapped her wings and flew out the window. But Blu's weight quickly dragged them down. He had to tell Jewel an embarrassing secret: He couldn't fly.

"*WHAT!*" squawked Jewel as they tumbled to the ground. "But you're a bird!"

Blu and Jewel managed to get away from Nigel and the smugglers. But they were still chained together.

When they found out that Blu and Jewel were gone, Linda and Tulio began desperately looking for them. Fernando felt bad about stealing the macaws, so he offered to help.

But they weren't the only ones searching for the missing birds. Nigel was after Blu and Jewel, too!

Rafael, a friendly toucan, knew someone who could help Blu and Jewel unlock the chain. It was a bulldog mechanic named Luiz.

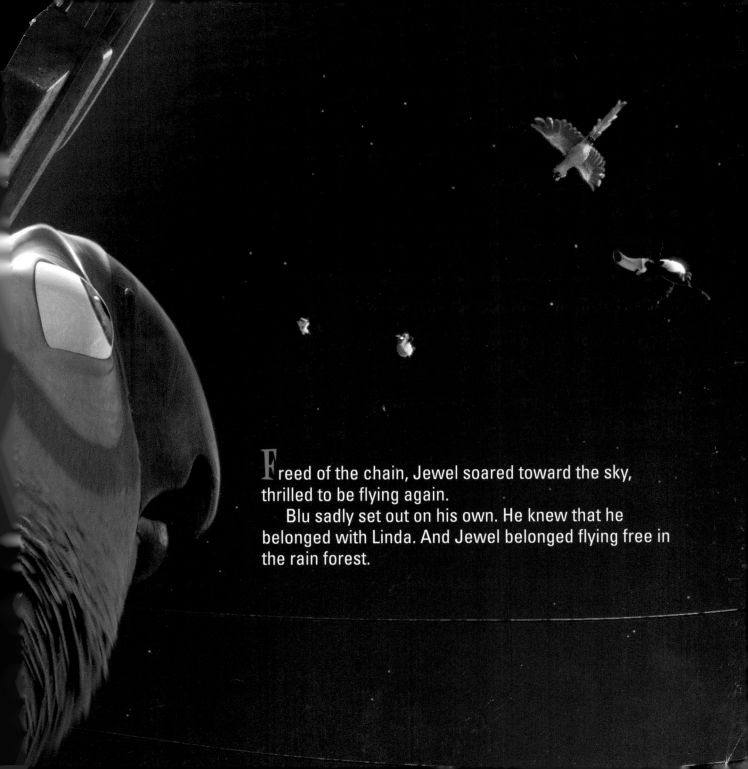

Freed of the chain, Jewel soared toward the sky, thrilled to be flying again.

Blu sadly set out on his own. He knew that he belonged with Linda. And Jewel belonged flying free in the rain forest.

Suddenly Nigel swooped down and grabbed Jewel! He brought her to Marcel, who was using a parade float to sneak all the stolen birds out of town.

As soon as Blu heard that Jewel had been captured, he rushed to find the float. But Nigel caught him in another cage! Soon Jewel and Blu were on a plane, flying away from Rio to be sold.

Thinking fast, Blu toppled his cage and it crashed open. He quickly freed all the other birds. But a cage had fallen on Jewel, injuring her wing and making it impossible for her to fly. And now the plane was plummeting to the ground!

"Go, Blu!" Jewel pleaded. "Save yourself!"
"I'm not leaving you," Blu replied.
Blu knew there was only way to save Jewel.

Blu learned to fly! He carried Jewel to safety.
Now he could stay in Rio forever.